To Moby and all creatures of the deep,
the high, and the wild, and
to all warriors
coping with our
insatiable,
endangered
humankind.
—EY

"It drifted down like soot, like snow,
In the dream-tossed Bronx, in the long ago...."

To Naomi Replansky, whose poetry has forever
inspired me.
—BD

ABOUT THIS BOOK
This book was edited by Alvina Ling and designed by David Caplan and Nicole Brown. The production was supervised by Ruiko Tokunaga, and the production editor was Jen Graham. The text was set in Gill Sans. The illustrations for this book were done in cut-paper collage.

Copyright © 2017 by Ed Young • Illustrations copyright © 2017 by Ed Young • Text copyright © 2017 by Barbara DaCosta • Cover art copyright © 2017 by Ed Young • Cover copyright © 2017 Hachette Book Group, Inc. • All rights reserved. In accordance with the U.S. Copyright Act of 1976, the scanning, uploading, and electronic sharing of any part of this book without the permission of the publisher is unlawful piracy and theft of the author's intellectual property. If you would like to use material from the book (other than for review purposes), prior written permission must be obtained by contacting the publisher at permissions@hbgusa.com. Thank you for your support of the author's rights. • Little, Brown and Company • Hachette Book Group • 1290 Avenue of the Americas, New York, NY 10104 • Visit us at lb-kids.com • Little, Brown and Company is a division of Hachette Book Group, Inc. • The Little, Brown name and logo are trademarks of Hachette Book Group, Inc. • The publisher is not responsible for websites (or their content) that are not owned by the publisher. • First Edition: June 2017 • Library of Congress Cataloging-in-Publication Data • Young, Ed, author. • Mighty Moby / Ed Young; text by Barbara DaCosta. — First edition. • pages cm • Summary: The classic tale of the hunt for Moby Dick, the whale, with a new twist. • ISBN 978-0-316-29936-7 (hardcover : alk. paper) 1. Whales—Juvenile fiction. 2. Bedtime—Juvenile fiction. [1. Whales—Fiction. 2. Bedtime—Fiction.] I. DaCosta, Barbara, author. II. Title. • PZ7.Y855Mi 2017 • [E]—dc23 • 2015020870 • 10 9 8 7 6 5 4 3 2 1 • APS • PRINTED IN CHINA

mighty moby

ED YOUNG

TEXT BY BARBARA DACOSTA

LITTLE, BROWN AND COMPANY
New York   Boston

"Three long years we've been at sea,
Homeward bound we want to be,
A-sailing, sailing, a-sailing-oh...."

"But keep an eye out for the prey,
Till Captain makes that big whale pay,
    A-sailing, sailing, a-sailing-oh."

"There
she blows!"
hollered the lookout.

"I'll get thee," the captain shouted at the distant whale, "if it's the last thing I do!"

"To your boats— we'll give chase!"

"Hurry, my sailors! Hurry!

"Row quiet....

Row fast....

Hold steady now—"

With a

WHOOSH,

the captain let fly
his harpoon.

The whale leaped away, boat in tow, and with a toss of its mighty tail

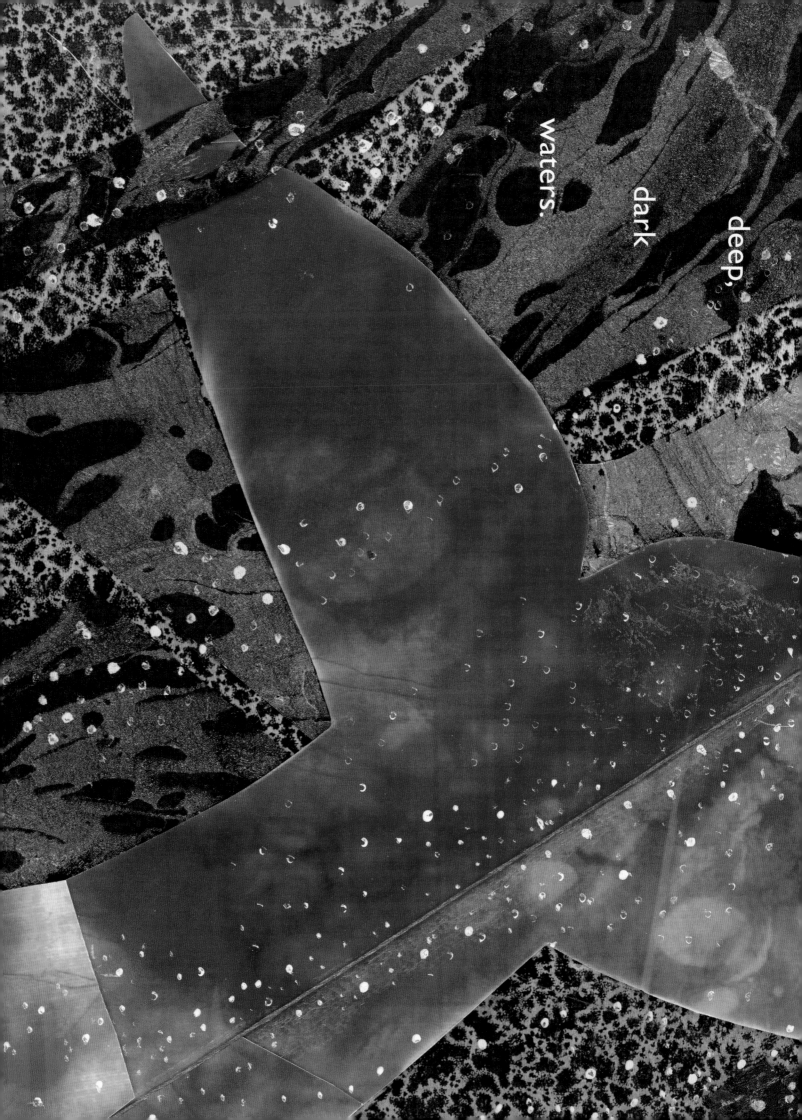

deep,

dark

waters.

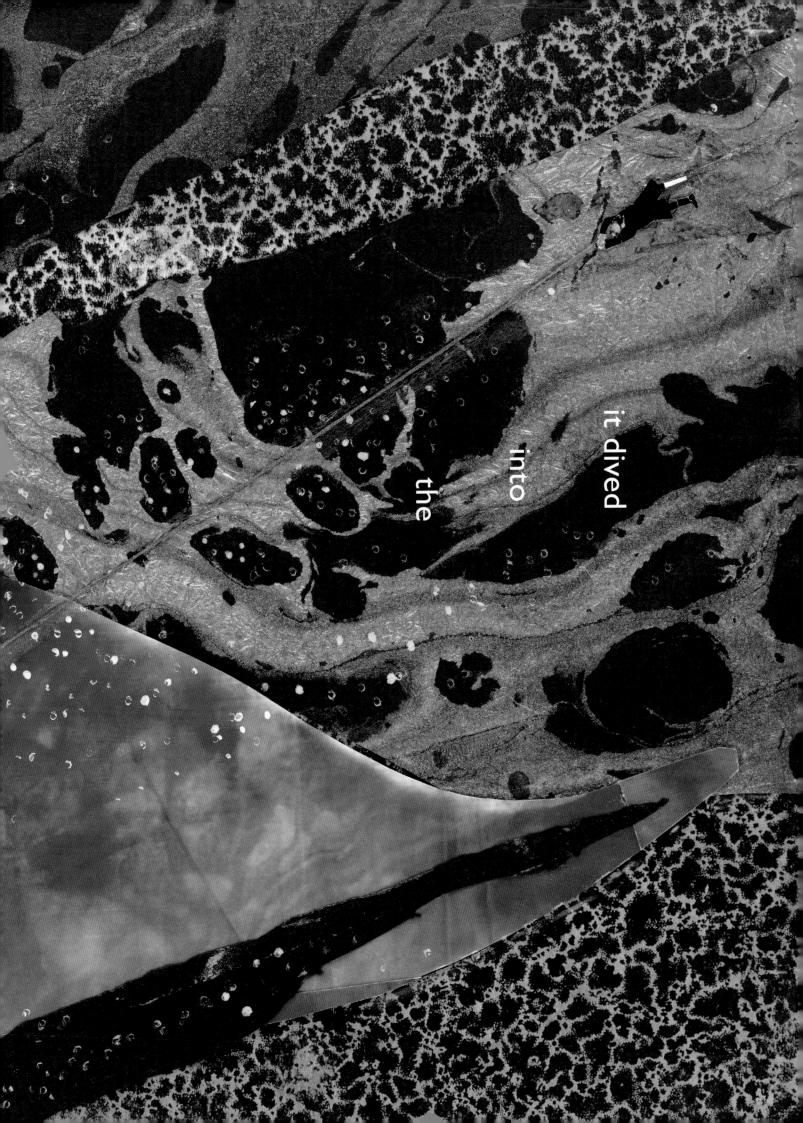

it dived

into

the

The sailors sat

scared and silent,

as the whaleboats rocked

upon the rolling waves,

when came

a rumbling

a rushing

an

earthquake

rising

from

the

deep—

THE

WHALE!

"HEY!"

HOT

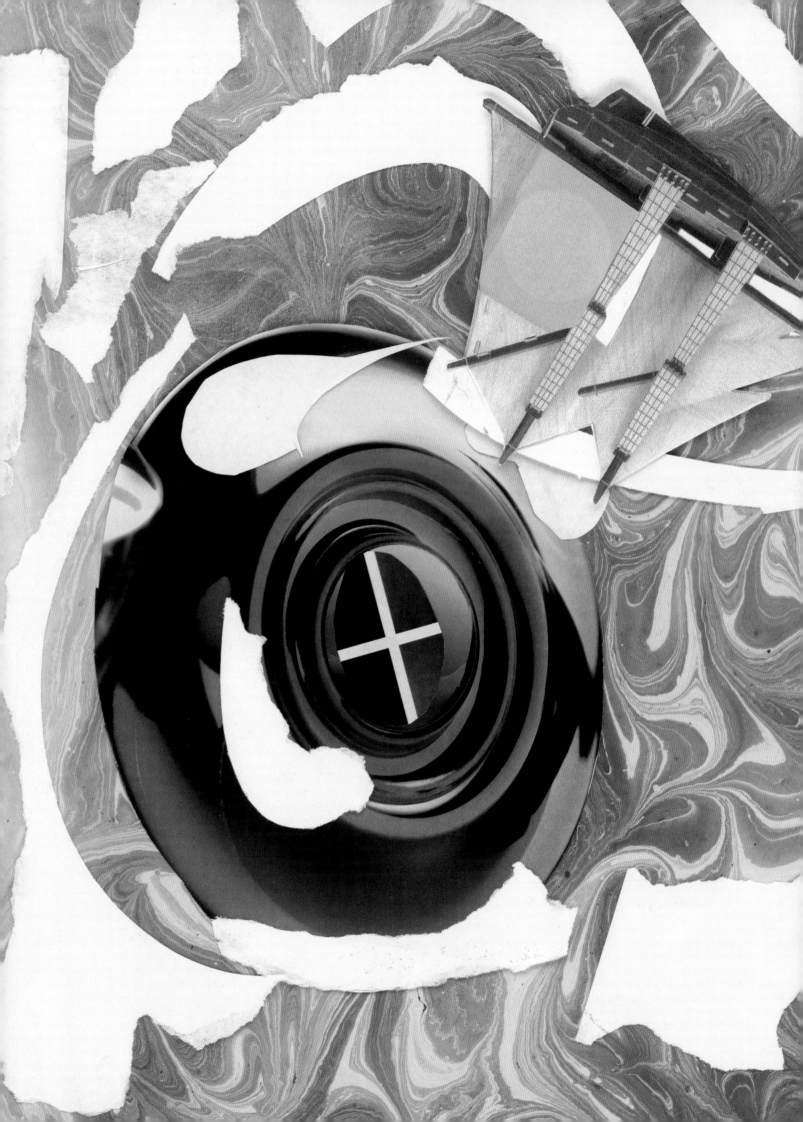

"My story's not done yet!"

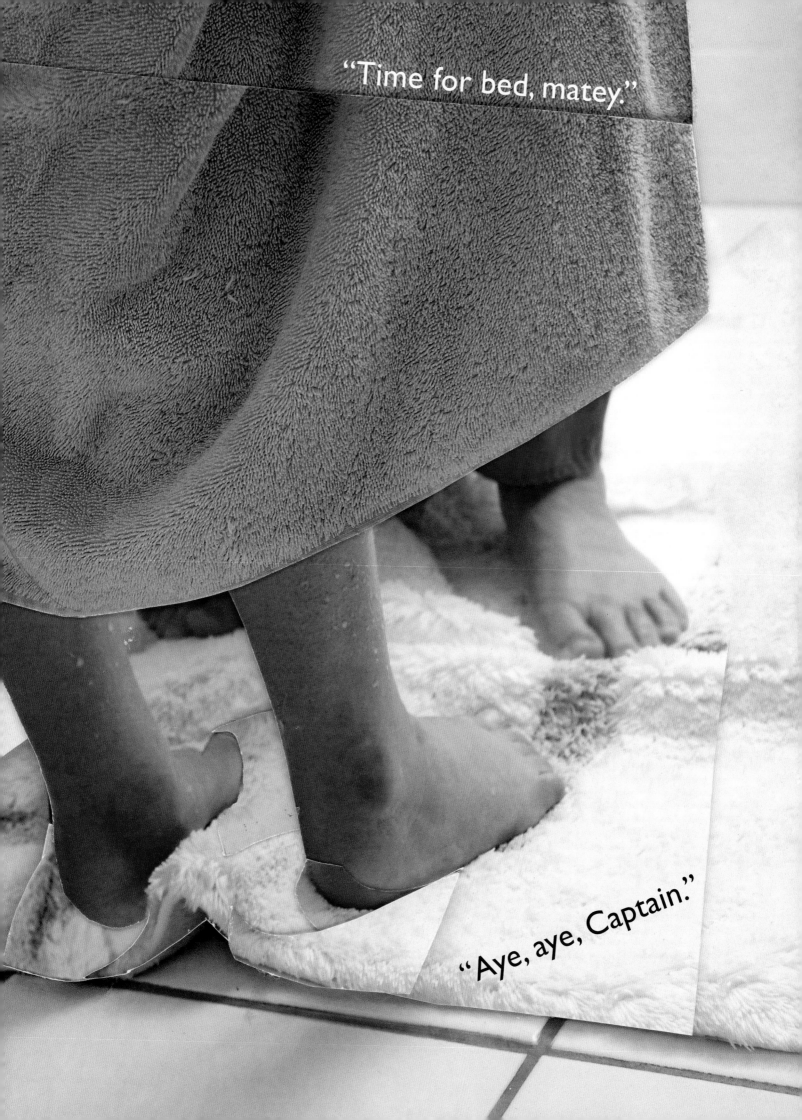

"Good night, little sailor."

"Sing me a song? Please?"

"All right...."

"Wide are the waters of the deep blue sea,
Great is the whale that got away free.

"Sleepy is the sailor who's tucked in bed,
Soft is the pillow beneath the young sailor's head."

AUTHORS' NOTE

Mighty Moby was inspired by the famous book *Moby Dick*, written by Herman Melville (1819–1891) and published in 1851. The story of Captain Ahab's obsessive chase after the whale who'd maimed him, *Moby Dick* is a window into a world of the past, yet is filled with issues still vital to our lives. The book became one of America's most important and influential novels, inspiring films, plays, operas, art, music, poems, comics, and many other works.

We used an unusual method for creating *Mighty Moby:* We worked "backward." Ed first created the story in drawings, and then Barbara wrote words to go with the pictures. Ed's final artwork was done in mixed-media collage, using cut paper, photographs, string, and pastel. Barbara employed a similar method for the text. She used some of the many styles of writing found in *Moby Dick*, and drew all but one of her words from it (readers will have to figure out which one it is!). The verses in *Mighty Moby* are modeled on sea chanteys and ballads. The opening verses can be sung to the chantey "Haul on the Bowline," and the last verse can be sung to the famous ballad "Lord Franklin." To all of this we added an element of childhood adventure-fantasy that we first explored in our previous collaboration, *Nighttime Ninja*.

For information, activities, and resources about *Mighty Moby* and *Moby Dick*, Herman Melville, whales, whaling, maritime music, and sailing, you can visit our website, www.mightymoby.wordpress.com.

We hope that if you enjoyed *Mighty Moby*, someday you'll also enjoy the adventure of reading *Moby Dick*!

Ed Young
Barbara DaCosta

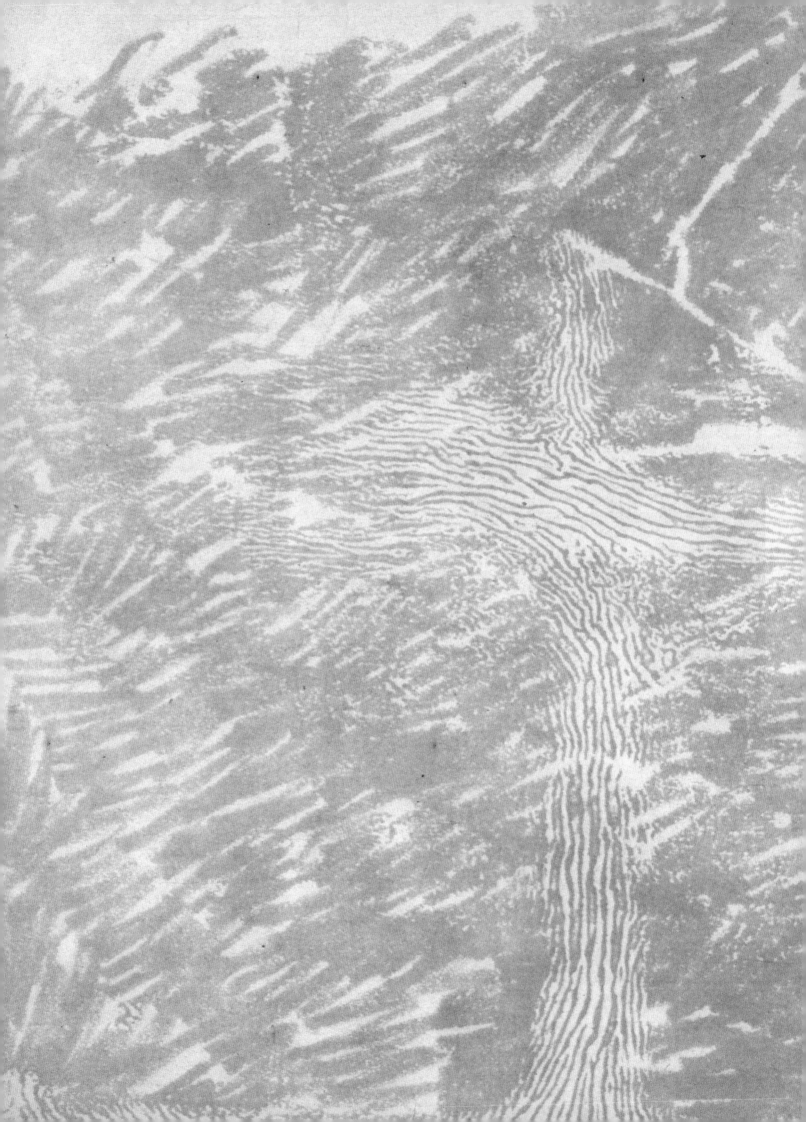